# ed vere

# HOW TO BE A
# LION

The world is full of ideas.

Big ones,
small ones.
Good ones,
bad ones.

Some think this . . .

others think that.

PUFFIN

Some say,

there's only **one** way to be a lion.

They say . . .

# Lions are FIERCE!

If they catch you
they will chomp you.

**Crunch,**

**crunch,**

**CHOMP!**

They say a lion can't be gentle.

Well, *they* haven't met Leonard.

Leonard loves to walk by himself,
feeling the sun warm his back
and the grass under his paws.

Some days Leonard walks to his thinking hill.

Sometimes he thinks important thoughts . . .
　　　　　Sometimes he daydreams.


Somewhere in between,
　　　he hums quietly and plays with words.
Putting them together
　　　this way, then that way —
　　　　　making them into poems.

Some say,

## WAIT!

Lions are **not** gentle!

Lions do **not** write poems!

And if a lion met a duck . . .

Bad luck for that duck.

**Crunch,**

**crunch,**

**CHOMP!**

But if Leonard met a duck . . .

What do **you** think would happen?

"Hello," said Leonard. "I'm Leonard."

"Hello," said the duck. "I'm Marianne."

"I'm writing a poem," said Leonard,
"but I'm stuck. Will you help me?"

"You're in luck," said Marianne.
"I'm a poetic duck."

Together,
they played with Leonard's poem,
until the words came unstuck.

Leonard and Marianne found they liked each other.

Under the sun, in the long grass, they lay together.

They played.

They went for walks
and had long meandering conversations,
a mixture of quacks and quiet roars.

At night they watched for shooting stars,
and made wishes if they saw them.

"Do you think the universe has edges?"
quacked Marianne.

"If it doesn't," said Leonard,
"will we fall out?"

Together they are happy.
They wish for nothing more than this.

(Some say that a lion should have chomped a duck by now . . .)

One day a pack of fierce lions came
prowling around.

"What's going on here?" they growled.
"Why hasn't this duck
          been chomped?"

"This duck is Marianne," said Leonard.
"She's my friend and nobody will chomp her!"

The fierce lions came closer.

"We heard you're gentle.
We heard you make up poems.
But not chomping a duck?
You've gone **too** far!"

The fierce lions growled and roared . . .

"There's only **one** way to be a lion . . .

Leonard,
        you **must** be fierce!"

"Must I be fierce?"
said Leonard.

"Must I change?"

"They're wrong!" quacked Marianne.
"And we will show them why."

Leonard and Marianne went to their thinking hill.
They thought hard.

After a while Leonard hummed a serious hum.
An idea started to form.

Marianne quacked a serious quack.
The idea grew.

They put their words together,
like this, like that, building them into a poem
        that made sense of what they thought.

Finally they were ready.

Leonard took a deep breath . . .

*"I'll say this quietly,*
*I needn't roar to be heard,*
*I can be a friend*
*to a bee or a bird.*

*You said I must change, I must chomp Marianne,*
*but chomping your friends is a terrible plan.*

Let nobody say
just **one** way is true.
There are so many ways
that you can be you.

If there **must** be a must,
then this we must try . . .

Why don't you, be **you** . . .

And I, will be **I**."

Some say words can't change the world.
Leonard says, if they make you think,
then maybe they can.

Is there just **one** way to be a lion?

I don't think so . . .

Do you?

*This book is for those who daydream,*
*and those who think for themselves.*

With thanks to Andrea MacDonald, Goldy Broad and Frances Gilbert.
And to Sophie Darlington for a place to stay full of inspiration.

PUFFIN BOOKS
UK | USA | Canada | Ireland | Australia | India | New Zealand | South Africa
Puffin Books is part of the Penguin Random House group of companies
whose addresses can be found at global.penguinrandomhouse.com.
www.penguin.co.uk   www.puffin.co.uk   www.ladybird.co.uk
First published 2018
Copyright © Ed Vere, 2018
The moral right of the author/illustrator has been asserted
Printed in China      001
A CIP catalogue record for this book is available from the British Library
Hardback ISBN: 978–0–141–37635–6
Paperback ISBN: 978–0–141–37636–3
All correspondence to: Puffin Books, Penguin Random House Children's
80 Strand, London WC2R 0RL

FSC
www.fsc.org
MIX
Paper from
responsible sources
FSC® C018179

www.edvere.com          @ed_vere

Lions are endangered. You can help them here:
www.ruahacarnivoreproject.com  &  www.lionguardians.org
Thank you!